The Good Samaritans

Tessa Krailing

WELLINGTON SQUARE

Contents

Tony gets a job

Mrs Potts had asked Tony and Tessa to do
some shopping for her.
It was Saturday morning and the shops were full.
'Have we got everything?' asked Tony.
'I think so,' said Tessa, looking at
the shopping list.
'Yes, that's everything. We can go home now.'
'Just a minute,' said Tony.
'I want to look in the window of the music shop.'
Tessa followed him over to the music shop.

'Look at that guitar,' said Tony.
'I'd love a guitar like that.'
'But you've got a guitar,' said Tessa.
'Oh, yes,' said Tony.
'But it's not a very good one.
I could play really well with that guitar.'
The twins looked at the guitar in the
window of the music shop.
'It's lovely,' said Tessa, 'but look at the price!'
'Yes, I know,' said Tony. 'It's a lot of money.
I haven't got nearly enough to buy it.'
Tony could have stayed in front of the window
looking at the guitar all day, but
Tessa said they had to get home.

Suddenly, Tessa stopped in front of
the newspaper shop.
'Tony!' she called. 'Come here and
look at this notice.'
Tony came over and looked at the notice
in the window of the newspaper shop.
It said, GIRL OR BOY WANTED FOR PAPER ROUND.
'What about it?' asked Tony.
'Stupid!' said Tessa.
'Go in and ask for the job.
Doing a paper round is easy, and you can
save your money and buy the guitar!'
'Oh yes,' said Tony. 'Good thinking.'

The twins went into the shop.
Mr Flint was seeing to other people so
the twins looked around.
The shop had sweets and toys
as well as newspapers.
A boy was talking to Mr Flint.
'Do you think he's asking for the job?'
said Tony, worried.
'No,' said Tessa. 'He's just bought some sweets.'

When the other people had left the shop,
the twins went over to Mr Flint.
'Yes,' he said, 'what can I do for you?'
'I've come about the notice in the window,'
said Tony.
'I'd like the job.'
'Oh,' said Mr Flint. 'You want to do the paper round?
Have you asked your Mum and Dad?'
'No,' said Tony. 'I never thought about that.'
'Well, ask your Mum and Dad, and if it's
all right with them, come back and
see me,' said Mr Flint.

The twins went back home and told
their Mum and Dad about the job.
'OK,' said Mrs Potts.
'I'll telephone Mr Flint and let him know
it's all right.
You go back to the shop and find out
what time you have to be there.'

Tony went back to the newspaper shop.
Mr Flint was just putting down the telephone
when Tony walked in.

'That was your Mum,' he said.
'She says it's all right so you can
start on Monday morning.
Be here at 7 o'clock.
If you're late, you don't keep the job. OK?'
'Yes, Mr Flint,' said Tony.

When Tony got back home Tessa was
waiting for him.
'Well?' she asked. 'Did you get the job?'
'Yes,' said Tony, 'but I'll never keep it!'
'Why not?' asked Tessa.
'I have to be there at 7 o'clock
every morning,' said Tony.
'You know I'm no good at getting up in
the morning and 7 o'clock is so early.'
'If you want enough money to buy your guitar
you'll just have to try,' said Tessa.
'I'll help you. I'll get up in the morning
and do the paper round with you.'
'Really?' said Tony, looking happier.
'That's great. I just might keep the job and
get enough money to buy the guitar.'

The first day

On Monday morning Tessa woke up at 6 o'clock.
She looked out of the window.
It looked as if it might rain.
'I'll just have a few more minutes in bed,'
she said to herself.
Soon Tessa was asleep again.
When she woke up again it was nearly 7 o'clock!
She jumped out of bed and ran into Tony's room.
'Wake up! Wake up!' she shouted.
Tony didn't move so she shook him hard.
'What is it?' said Tony, sitting up quickly.
He was still half asleep and he didn't
remember that it was the first day of his job.
'Get up!' said Tessa. 'Come on!
You're going to be late for the paper round!'
'Oh, no!' said Tony.
'Quick,' said Tessa. 'Get your clothes on.
We'll have to run all the way there.'

When Tony and Tessa got to the newspaper shop
they were out of breath.
'Five minutes late!' said Mr Flint.
'That's not a very good start.'
'Sorry,' said Tony.
'Well, see it doesn't happen again,' said Mr Flint.
'Next time you're late you'll lose your job.
Now here's the bag of newspapers.
The number of the house is on the top
of each paper.'
'Right,' said Tony.
'Well, don't just stand there,' said Mr Flint.
'You're late already. Get a move on.'

Tony went quickly out of the shop.
Tessa was waiting for him outside.
They went round the Square putting
the newspapers through the letter-boxes.
'Here's a paper for Mrs Nash,' said Tessa.
'I remember Mrs Nash.
She's the old lady we took the letter to.
She lives all alone.
Let's knock on the door and say hello.'

Tessa knocked on the door of number 23.
She saw the curtains move and Mrs Nash looked out.
When she saw it was the twins, she came and
opened the door.
'Hello, Mrs Nash,' said Tony.
'Do you remember us?'
'Yes,' said Mrs Nash, smiling.
'I remember you. You found a letter I'd dropped
in the park and you brought it to me.
I remember you had on those strange masks.
You gave me a terrible fright.'

The twins told Mrs Nash about Tony's job and
about the guitar.
Suddenly Tessa remembered the time.
She looked at her watch.
'We'll have to go,' she said.
'We must finish this paper round.'

Tony and Tessa finished the paper round
and went back to the shop with the empty bag.
Mr Flint was waiting for them.
He looked at his watch and then at the twins.
'You've been a very long time,' he said.
'All the other kids came back ages ago.
You'll have to be quicker if you want to
keep the job!'

Tony gave the empty bag back to Mr Flint and
the twins went off to school.
'We're going to be late for school,' said Tony.
'Yes,' said Tessa. 'Mr Belter isn't going
to be very pleased.'

Tessa was right!
Mr Belter wasn't pleased at all.
'You're late,' he said to the twins as
they came into the classroom.
'We've been doing our paper round,' said Tony.
'If your paper round makes you late for school
you'd better stop doing it,' said Mr Belter.
'Now sit down and get your books out.'

Mrs Nash needs help

It was the end of the week.
Tony had been a paper boy for five days but
he still couldn't wake up early.
Every morning Tessa had to get him up.
On Friday, he was almost late again.
'Just made it on time,' said Mr Flint.
'Good job you did!'
Tony picked up the heavy bag of newspapers and
left the shop.

When the twins reached number 23, they were
surprised that Mrs Nash wasn't there to say hello.
'She might still be asleep,' said Tessa.
'No, she's always up early,' said Tony.
'I think there's something wrong.'

'Look at that milk bottle on the doorstep,'
said Tony.
'The milkman doesn't get here this early.
It must be left over from yesterday.'
'Do you think she's gone away for
a few days?' asked Tessa.
'No,' said Tony. 'She would have told us.
She would have asked us not to bring
her newspaper.'
'Do you think she's ill?' asked Tessa.
'We'd better find out,' said Tony.

He knocked on the door and shouted through
the letter-box.
'Mrs Nash, are you all right?'
The twins listened, but they couldn't hear
any sound inside the house.
'Let's look through the window,' said Tessa.
'Yes,' said Tony. 'I'm sure something's wrong.'
Tessa looked through the window.
'I can see her!' she called.
'She's on the floor. I think she's hurt!
What shall we do?' she said.

'We can't get in,' said Tony, 'so we'd
better get help.'
The twins ran to Kevin's house.
They told Kevin's Dad about Mrs Nash.
'I'll call the police,' said Mr Miller.
'It looks as if we'll need an ambulance as well.'

The police came quickly and the ambulance
was there soon after.
PC Kent had to break the door down before
he could get in.
'You stay here,' he said to the twins.
Tony and Tessa waited outside.
'I hope she's all right,' said Tessa.

The ambulance men followed PC Kent into the
house with a stretcher.
They brought out Mrs Nash on the stretcher.
'Is she badly hurt?' asked Tessa.
'I think she's broken her leg,' said PC Kent.
'It looks as if she fell down the stairs.
The poor old lady must have been on the floor
for hours.
What made you look through the window anyway?'

'We bring her newspaper,' said Tony.
'She always comes to the door and says hello.
When she didn't come this morning and
we saw yesterday's milk on the doorstep,
we knew something was wrong.'
'Well, it's a good job you did,' said PC Kent.
'We could do with more kids like you around.'

Trouble for the twins!

Tony and Tessa watched the policeman
get into his car.
Suddenly Tessa remembered the papers.
'We've still got some papers,' she said.
'Quick! We'd better finish the paper round and
get back to the shop or we'll be in trouble.
Mr Flint isn't going to be too pleased,'
said Tony.

Tony was right.
Mr Flint was not very pleased.
'My telephone has been ringing and
ringing,' he said.
'People asking for their newspapers.
What have you been doing all this time?'
'We're late because...' began Tony.
'I don't want to hear,' said Mr Flint.
'Just give me the bag and don't come here again.
I'll find another paper boy!'

When the twins got to school they were
in trouble with Mr Belter.
'Why are you so late?' he asked.
'Please Mr Belter...' began Tessa.
'I don't want to hear,' said Mr Belter crossly.
'You'll have to stay in after school and
catch up on the work you've missed.'

Rocky and Ben stayed after school to
talk to the twins.
'What happened?' asked Ben.
The twins told them about Mrs Nash and
how Tony had lost his job.
'Now I'll never get the guitar,' said Tony.

The twins finished their work and left school.
When they got home, PC Kent was there.
He was telling Mr and Mrs Potts all about
how the twins had helped Mrs Nash.
'She's doing well in hospital,' said PC Kent,
'thanks to the twins' quick thinking.'

Mr and Mrs Potts were pleased that the twins
had helped the old lady.
'That was a good thing to do,' said Mr Potts.
'Yes,' said Tony. 'You think so, and so does PC Kent,
but we're in trouble with Mr Flint and Mr Belter.
I've lost my job because we took so long over
the paper round and Mr Belter made us stay
in after school because we were late.'
'Did you tell them what happened?'
asked Mrs Potts.
'We tried to, but they wouldn't listen,' said Tony.
'Well, you know you did the right thing,'
said Mr Potts.

The next day was Saturday, so the twins went
to the hospital to see Mrs Nash.
She was pleased to see them.
'I must thank you for helping me,' she said.
'Just like Good Samaritans.
It didn't make you late with your paper round, did it?'
Tony and Tessa looked at each other.
'I don't do the paper round now,' said Tony.
'I didn't like getting up so early.'
He didn't tell Mrs Nash he had lost his job.
He didn't want to upset her.

Rocky and Ben help out

On Monday morning Tessa was pleased that
she didn't have to wake Tony up early.
But Tony was unhappy because he would never
get his guitar now.

At school that day Rocky and Ben talked
about what had happened.
'Tony is really fed up because he can't have his
guitar,' said Rocky.
'I know,' said Ben, 'but I've thought
of a way to help him.'

After school Rocky and Ben went round
the Square with Rocky's money box.
They told people about how the twins
had helped Mrs Nash and how Tony lost his job.
'We want to buy a new guitar for Tony,' said Ben.
'Will you please give us some money?'
People were glad to help.

Mr Patel said he would put a box in his shop.
'People will see the box when they come shopping,'
he said.
'I'm sure everyone will give some money.'

Rocky and Ben went into the newspaper shop.
Mr Flint had heard how the twins helped Mrs Nash.
'I'm sorry I wouldn't let him go on doing the
paper round,' he said.
'Tony tried to tell me what happened but
I wouldn't listen.
That was stupid of me.'
He opened the till and took out a £5 note.
'I'll put a box by my till in my shop and
I'll put £5 in myself,' he said.

'Everyone's given money,' said Rocky.
'They all know that Tony helped Mrs Nash.
They call the twins the Good Samaritans.'
'There's a lot of money here,' said Ben.
'How much is the guitar?'
'I don't know,' said Rocky.
'We'll have to ask in the music shop.'

All the kids went to the shop.
They looked at the price of the guitar
in the window.
'Look at the price!' said Rocky.
'We don't have enough to buy it.'
'Well, let's go in and see what
Mrs Chant has got,' said Ben.

Rocky told Mrs Chant about how they had
asked people for money so that they could
buy Tony the guitar in the shop window.
'We've got £40,' said Ben.
'Have you got a guitar for £40?'
'I know Tony Potts,' said Mrs Chant.
'I heard how the twins helped Mrs Nash.
He should have a good guitar.
You can have the one in the window
for £40.'

Rocky and the others went to the twins' house.
They hid the guitar behind them and Ben
knocked on the door.
When Tony opened the door all the kids
shouted 'Surprise!' and cheered loudly.
Rocky gave Tony the guitar.
'It's from everyone in the Square,' he said.
'They all gave money to buy it for you.'
Tony was so surprised he couldn't say anything.
He just couldn't believe the guitar was his.

'Play us something,' said Ben.
'Yes, play us something,' said the others.
Tony began to play his new guitar.
The kids thought it was great.

Tony took the guitar to show Tessa and his
Mum and Dad.
'Let's play something together,' said Tessa.
'OK,' said Mr Potts.
Tessa played the drums.
Mr Potts played the trumpet and Mrs Potts
played another guitar.

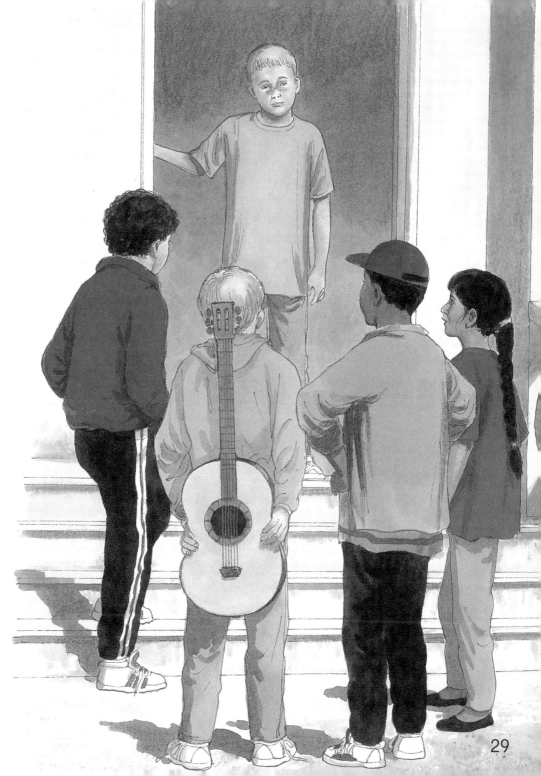

'You know,' said Ben,
'I think Mrs Nash would like to hear you play.
She'll be so pleased you got your guitar.'
'We could go to the hospital and play for her,'
said Tony.
'Now wait a minute,' said Mr Potts.
'I'm sure the doctor wouldn't like us all
going to the hospital.
Mrs Nash needs to be quiet so that she
can get better.
We'll wait until she comes home, then
we'll play for her.'
'Yes,' said Tessa. 'We could play in the Square.
Then everyone who gave money for the guitar can
listen to the music.'

Soon Mrs Nash came out of hospital.
She had hurt her leg badly so the doctor said
she shouldn't walk for a few days.
The twins helped her out again by pushing
her around the Square.

The first time they did this
they had a big surprise for her.
They took her to the statue of the Duke of Wellington.
All her friends were waiting there.
And there was Mr Potts with his trumpet, and
Mrs Potts with her guitar.
All the Potts family played for Mrs Nash.
Tony and Mrs Potts played their guitars,
Mr Potts played the trumpet and
Tessa played the drums.

'What a lovely noise,' said Mrs Nash.
'I've never heard anything like it.
You've really cheered me up, you know.
You're still my Good Samaritans.'